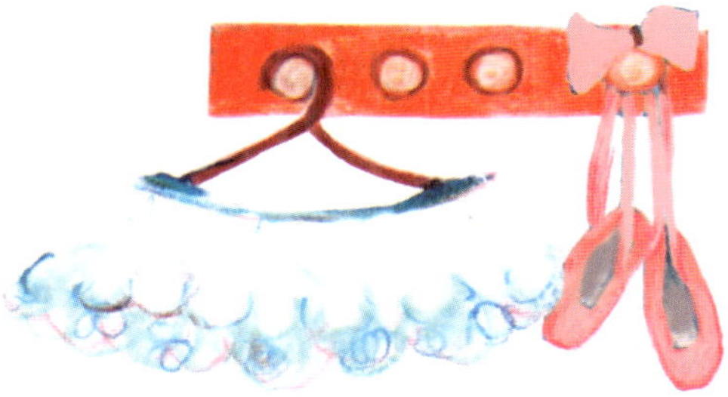

Bear's Perfect Dance

A book to share from
Scallywag Press

To Tony, Will, Maddie and Mei, who remind me to embrace the joy and freedom of the imperfect dance

First published in Great Britain in 2026
by Scallywag Press Ltd, 10 Sutherland Row, London SW1V 4JT

Printed in China by Toppan Leefung

001

British Library Cataloguing in Publication Data available
ISBN 978–1–836300–40–3

FSC www.fsc.org MIX Paper | Supporting responsible forestry FSC® C104723

Bear's Perfect Dance

Rachel Tilda Wolf

Scallywag Press Ltd
LONDON

Bear loved to dance.

He practised all day long . . .

He touched
his toes,

concentrated on
his balance

and mastered
the splits.

His dance moves were perfect!

But something bothered Bear – he was lonely, always dancing by himself . . .

and some dances were
better with two.

So Bear decided to find
a dance partner . . .

the PERFECT
dance partner!

Who would be the perfect dance partner?

Bear made a checklist.

Then he made some posters.

Bear put them up
all around the forest.

WANTED
A Dance Partner for Bear
is it you?
DITIONS TOMORROW

The next morning, Bear had butterflies in his tummy he was so excited!

He put on his favourite tutu and picked his best ballet pumps.

Then he did some warm-ups

and reread his checklist.

But what if no-one had seen his posters?
What if no-one came to audition?

Anxiously, Bear
opened the door . . .

The garden was full of
woodland animals, eager to
show off their favourite moves.

First to audition was Crow . . .

but her Can-Can
was chaotic.

Beaver's Boogie
had no Woogie.

Snake's Shimmy
was too slithery.

There was no fandango
in Fox's Flamenco.

And Wild Pig's Waltz
was ever-so awkward.

Then, Stag
struck a pose
and . . .

just stood there!

But there was no ‘next’ . . .

The waiting animals had grown bored and had wandered off.

Bear was heartbroken.

Slowly, he trailed back indoors,
his hopes dashed.

I'll never find the perfect dance partner, he thought.
I'll never dance the perfect dance.

Then he heard
something . . .

KNOCK

KNOCK

KNOCK

Bear was curious,
who could it be?

A child was dancing outside,
twisting and turning,
swirling and twirling.

As Bear watched, he felt
his heart begin to mend . . .

It wasn't like any dance he had seen before –
but there was **something** about it . . .

it was full of
JOY!

"Hello," said the child, noticing Bear at last.
"Am I too late for the audition?
I hope not because I love to dance."

"So do I," said Bear, "and I'd love to learn
your dance. Will you teach me?"

"I'd like that very much!"
said the child.

Shyly, at first, Bear copied the child's moves –
not perfectly, but clumsily . . .

then more freely and joyfully as they
danced their dance together.

The animals were watching Bear learn these new moves. They wanted to try them too . . .

"Come join us!" called Bear to them all.

So they did!

It was messy,
it was muddlesome,
jubilant and joyful.

Together, they danced to the
music in their hearts . . .

. . . and it was **perfect!**